Stephanie
from: Neal + Gina

maggie

*for Odile Anderson* —S.K.

*for Mary Kuritz* —T.H.

# DIRTY FEET

by Steven Kroll

pictures by Toni Hormann

PARENTS MAGAZINE PRESS
NEW YORK

Library of Congress Cataloging in Publication Data
Kroll, Steven.       Dirty feet.
SUMMARY: Penelope removes her too-tight sneakers
on the way to school, thereby setting the stage for
a series of disastrous encounters between her feet
and a variety of messy substances.
[ 1. Shoes and boots—Fiction.      2. Cleanliness—Fiction]
I. Hormann, Toni.  II. Title.  PZ7.K9225Di  [E]  80–17570
ISBN 0–8193–1035–2     ISBN 0–8193–1036–0 (lib. bdg.)

Penelope had three pairs of shoes.
There were the brown-and-white saddle shoes
and the black ones she wore for dress-up.
But the shoes she liked best
were the bright green sneakers
with the orange racing stripes.

She wore them to the park.
She wore them when she visited her friends.
And she wore them to school almost every day.
The trouble was, Penelope was growing
out of her favorite shoes.

One morning the sneakers felt
even tighter than usual.
But Penelope squeezed them on anyway
and dashed out the door to school.

It had rained during the night.
Puddles were everywhere.
Penelope was careful not to step in any.
The more she walked,
the tighter the sneakers felt.

Finally, she couldn't stand them anymore.
She had to take them off.
She undid the laces
and slipped her feet out.
"Whew! What a relief!" she said.

Suddenly a breeze came up
and blew off her hat.
She left her sneakers
and ran after it.

The hat landed in the middle
of a big mud puddle.
Penelope had no choice.
She waded in and pulled it out.
The mud felt cool and squishy.

Just then, the school bell rang.
Penelope ran back to get her sneakers.
They were gone!
It was too late to go home.
Her mother would be angry.

But how could she show up at school
without shoes?
Her teacher would be angry.
And worst of all, her favorite shoes
were lost.
Penelope was worried.

She walked through more puddles
without noticing them.
She walked through a pile

of garbage somebody had dumped,
and through little piles of dirt
left by a street cleaner.

Before she knew it, she was at school.
Everyone pointed and giggled,
even her friends Brenda and Tim.

Penelope kept her head high
and marched into her classroom.

"My goodness, Penelope,"
said Mrs. James, her teacher.
"Where are your shoes,
and why are your feet so dirty?"

Penelope didn't know what to say.

Would Mrs. James understand about
tight shoes and mud puddles?

"Penelope," said Mrs. James,
"go wash your feet.
Then we'll try to find
something to put on them."

Washing feet was fun...
until Penelope saw there were
no paper towels to dry them.

She tried to shake her feet dry...
but that didn't work.

"Dirty feet again," said Mrs. James.
"And dirty footprints in the hall!
Didn't you dry your feet after you washed them?"
"Couldn't," said Penelope. "No towels."

"My goodness. Tell Mr. Whitlock
to bring towels and a mop.
Then wash your feet again—and dry them—
and I'll keep looking for some shoes."

Mr. Whitlock was in the basement.
The stairs were dark.
The floor was dirty.
Penelope walked on her toes like a ballerina.
Mr. Whitlock was even dirtier than the floor.
He had been fixing the furnace.

Penelope delivered her message.
Mr. Whitlock got his mop
and set off upstairs.
Penelope tripped on the first step,
fell on a pile of greasy rags,
and wound up dirty head to toe.

Mrs. James shook her head.
"My goodness. You just get
dirtier and dirtier.

See if the lost-and-found box
has some shoes. I couldn't find any.
Then wash up the best you can
and come back to class."

The lost-and-found box was in the
waiting room outside the principal's office.
A painter had painted half the floor.
He'd gone out and forgotten to leave
a sign saying, "WET PAINT."

So Penelope didn't notice the paint
until her feet started to feel wet and sticky.
"Oh, boy," she thought, "this is it for sure!"
Just then, Mrs. Price, the principal,
appeared in the doorway.

She looked at Penelope.
Penelope looked at her.
And the two of them broke out laughing.
"Well, Penelope," Mrs. Price said finally.

"Mrs. James told me you were coming,
but I guess I didn't get here soon enough.
Let's get you cleaned up.
Then we'll look
in the lost-and-found box."

All Penelope and Mrs. Price found were
a Batman cape,
a hair barrette,
and a dried-up peanut-butter sandwich.

So Mrs. Price said,
"I'll give you an old pair of shoes
that I keep here for bad weather.
We'll stuff them with paper towels.
When you get home for lunch,
put your own shoes on.
And bring these back this afternoon."

Back in class, there was
more laughter.

Even Penelope joined in.
She had to admit her feet looked silly.

On the way home,
Penelope walked as quickly as she could
in Mrs. Price's shoes.
She stayed very far away from mud puddles.

When she reached her house,
the postman was there, too.
He pulled her sneakers out of his truck.
"I knew these were yours," he said.
"A dog left them under a tree."

Penelope thanked the postman,
put on her sneakers,
and carried Mrs. Price's shoes
into the house.
Her mother was there waiting.

"Why are you so dirty?" she said.
"And why are you carrying those old shoes?"
"It's a long story," said Penelope.
"I'll tell you during lunch."
"All right," said her mother.
"But first I have a surprise for you."

It was a new pair of sneakers,
exactly like her old ones—except they fit.

## ABOUT THE AUTHOR

STEVEN KROLL remembers the first time he was inspired to write a story: "I was thirteen. One rainy evening I was walking home. The street was shimmering, and I thought it looked like it was made of glass. I ran home and began to write a story about a world made of glass. When I finished, I discovered that in my hurry I had forgotten to wipe my shoes at the front door. There were dirty footprints, and I had to clean them up! Perhaps, on that evening so long ago, I had already found the beginnings of *Dirty Feet*."

Mr. Kroll grew up in New York and lives there now. But he has also lived in London and in Maine, where he began to write full time about ten years ago. Since then he has published more than a dozen children's books.

## ABOUT THE ARTIST

TONI HORMANN was born in Detroit and grew up in Chicago. "As a child," she says, "I lost hats, mittens, hankies, books, lunch money, and everything else not strapped, pinned, or tied to my body. But I never lost shoes. Now, through Penelope, I have."

Ms. Hormann has raised four children (all of whom lost many things while they were growing up). She now lives in Elmhurst, Illinois.

In addition to another picture book, Toni Hormann has illustrated text materials and children's games.

PARENTS MAGAZINE PRESS is pleased to welcome both STEVEN KROLL and TONI HORMANN to its group of authors and artists.